Kindness in words creates confidence.

Kindness in thinking creates profoundness.

Kindness in giving creates love.

-Lao Tzu

I dedicate this book to my grandchildren:
Jayde, Ariel, Aaron, Carter, Owen

-Judy Daniels Laird

My paintings are
dedicated to my five pixies:
Olivia, Ansel, Evan, Viola,
Noelle

-Deborah Smith

What Tilly Knows

A Pixie's Amazing Discovery

Insects
A-Z

Everything
You Need
To Know

Baggs Schrank

Written by

Judy Daniels Laird

Illustrated by

Deborah Smith

Once upon a time there was a wee pixie named Tilly.

She made her home in a lovely garden behind the Riley Museum.

Unlike other pixies, Tilly was shy. She was so timid that she kept to herself. She could have been quite lonely, if it weren't for her books.

She LOVED to read.

Tilly had discovered a Little Free Library that had been placed in the garden and she borrowed from it frequently.

Her books took her all over the world and she could find the answer to almost any question. Because Tilly read so many books, she knew a lot.

One evening around dusk, Tilly decided to stretch her legs and exercise her wings because she had been sitting and reading most of the day. She stood, took a few steps and flapped her wings. Off she flew through the garden.

Just as she was flying over the rose arbor, "CRASH." She had collided with something.

She looked up and heard someone say, "Hey, who are you? I haven't seen you around here before."

Small like Tilly, he was covered in brown feathers. He had big golden eyes and little tufts for ears.

In a soft voice, Tilly shyly answered, "I'm Tilly, and you are a screech owl even though you don't screech and you probably live in that hole in the big walnut tree over there."

"You're right," he smiled.

"How do you know so much about me?" he asked.

"Well," explained Tilly, "I read about owls in a book!"

"That's cool," he replied. "I am glad to meet you. I'm Silas."

After Tilly returned home, she thought about the little owl. She had enjoyed talking to him.

A few days later, Tilly was sitting outside when she was surprised to see Silas flying towards her.

"I've been looking for you, Tilly. I have a favorite branch in the redbud tree and every evening I go there and look down in the garden. Would you like to join me this evening?" Silas asked.

Tilly happily joined him. She noticed how Silas really listened when she talked and how kind he was to her.

In the days ahead, Tilly and Silas became friends. One morning they were talking when Lee, the honey bee, buzzed by. "Good morning, Lee. How are things?" Silas called out.

"Well, I have come into the garden looking for flowers to make honey and there are so many, I don't know which ones are the best," explained Lee.
"I see," replied Silas.
"I don't either but Tilly here may know."

Sure enough, Tilly knew a lot about bees and honey-making. In a more confident voice she said, "Bees are attracted to the color yellow for a reason. These sunflowers will make delicious honey."

"Bees also love the color purple and lavender makes wonderful honey, too. But the mint growing in the herb bed is the best option of all."

"Wow!" smiled Lee. "Thank you, Tilly!" He flew from flower to flower happily gathering pollen and nectar.

One evening, Silas said hello to Freddie, a young fire-fly. "Freddie, it's good to see you. How are you this evening?"

"Not so good. I am having trouble getting my light to come on," cried Freddie.

"Well, what could cause that, I wonder?" frowned Silas. Then he thought, let me ask Tilly. "I think I know the answer to your problem," smiled Tilly.

"The last few evenings have been chilly. Fireflies need warm nights to light up," she said. "Oh," replied Freddie. "I'm not so worried now."

"Summertime is almost here and my light should work fine. Thanks, Tilly," he said as he flew away. Silas looked at Tilly and winked.

"Your knowledge has helped many of our friends," he said. "Yes," thought Tilly. "They are my friends, too."

A few mornings later, when Tilly went to return a book, she noticed a stranger in the garden. Off she flew to wake up Silas.

"Silas, a CAT has come into the garden. What should we do?" You see, Tilly knew that pixies and owls were not usually friends with CATS!

Tilly and Silas sat high up in the redbud tree and watched the cat the rest of the day. He slinked under a large bush and meowed softly. His coat was a dirty yellow, he had big green eyes and his tail was crooked.

"I have never seen him before. Do you think he is lost?" muttered Tilly.

The next morning, the cat was still there. Tilly knew a lot about cats and something was not right!

Silas was worried for the little cat! He had been thinking of a plan and finally he whispered in Tilly's ear. She flew to the window of the museum.

She could see people inside, docents, who took visitors on tours of the museum.

Tilly wanted to get their attention. Quickly, she tapped on the window and hid. A docent turned around but didn't see anything. Tilly tapped again, louder this time.

The docent looked out and saw the cat sitting quietly under the bush.

"Oh hello, sweet kitty, what are you doing under that bush? Oh my," she moaned as she picked him up.

You are as light as a feather. I bet you are hungry."

She brought the little cat into the museum. He was an instant hit with the other docents.

They fed him and took turns holding him. It soon began to rain and they decided that they could not turn him out into the weather, so he spent the night in the museum.

The next morning when the docents arrived, the cat met them at the door with a mouse that he had caught during the night.

"Oh," they beamed.
"He is helping us keep the museum free of mice!"

So that is how Little Tom, as the docents called him, became a full-time resident of the museum. Little Tom finally had a home. It was a perfect fit for him."

One evening as Silas and Tilly were sitting in their favorite redbud tree, they looked into the window of the museum and saw Little Tom jump up on the window sill.

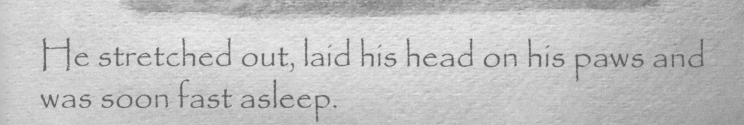

He stretched out, laid his head on his paws and was soon fast asleep.

"You know, Silas," Tilly said. You reached out to me when I needed someone. I've seen how caring you are with our friends, even Little Tom there. I know a lot of stuff, but you taught me how to be a friend."

And she gave her friend a hug!

Let's Talk... <small>Parents and Teachers</small>

What does it mean to be shy? How could you help someone who is shy?

How did Silas help Tilly?

How was Tilly able to help the friends in the garden?

Tilly had a little friend who followed her around on the pages of the story. Who was it?

Why did Silas ask Tilly to tap on the museum window?

What did Silas think Little Tom needed the most?

What does it mean to be kind?

How can you be more kind to others?

About the Riley Home

Tilly lives in the garden behind the James Whitcomb Riley Home and museum in Greenfield, Indiana.

Tours are given by the docents but visitors can explore the garden anytime to see a butterfly flower garden, a rose bed, pioneer garden and of course a pixie garden. You may want to come find Tilly and her friends or look in your own yard for other pixies!

About Little Free Libraries

Little Free Libraries can be found in many communities all over the world.

To find one in your area you can go to littlefreelibraries.org.

About the Author

If you stopped by Judy Laird's home in Indiana, chances are you would find her outside. Her love of nature led her to obtain Master Gardener and Master Naturalist certifications. Her story is patterned after Midwestern gardens and animals. She is a former elementary teacher with a Master's Degree.

Children today face many challenges that were unheard of a decade ago. They need our support and love more than ever. Kindness can change lives. This book is for every child who needs a friend.

About the Illustrator

Deborah Smith is a Kansas State University graduate with a Fine Arts degree. She now creates paintings in several mediums from her home in Noblesville, Indiana. She is a member of the Watercolor Society of Indiana, Indiana Asso. of Plein Air Painters, Nickel Plate Arts and is featured in the book "Indiana Painters of the 21st Century." She sings with the Indianapolis Symphonic Choir and is a Master Gardener and Member of the Hancock County Herb Society. You can see more of her art on Facebook at Sycamore Ridge Studio.

CPSIA information can be obtained
at www.ICGtesting.com
Printed in the USA
BVHW021953190821
614647BV00007B/33

* 9 7 8 0 9 9 9 8 5 0 7 8 7 *